# Two Sticks

Orel Protopopescu

Pictures by
Anne Wilsdorf

Melanie Kroupa Books
Farrar, Straus and Giroux • New York

To Claire Nicolas White, poet and dear friend
—O.P.

To a sweet little shrimp named Jacek
—A.W.

Text copyright © 2007 by Orel Protopopescu
Illustrations copyright © 2007 by Anne Wilsdorf
All rights reserved
Distributed in Canada by Douglas & McIntyre Ltd.
Color separations by Embassy Graphics
Printed and bound in China
Designed by Symon Chow
First edition, 2007
1 3 5 7 9 10 8 6 4 2

www.fsgkidsbooks.com

Library of Congress Cataloging-in-Publication Data
Protopopescu, Orel Odinov.
  Two sticks / Orel Protopopescu ; pictures by Anne Wilsdorf.— 1st ed.
    p.  cm.
  Summary: Maybelle loves to drum, but doesn't own a drum. After bringing home
eleven crocodiles in whose mouths she has played a toothy tune, her parents are only
too eager to replace them with any drum of Maybelle's choosing.
  ISBN-13: 978-0-374-38022-9
  ISBN-10: 0-374-38022-8
  [1. Drum—Fiction.  2. Crocodiles—Fiction.  3. Stories in rhyme.]  I. Wilsdorf, Anne, ill.
II. Title.

PZ8.3.P937Tw 2007
[E]—dc22
                                                                                        2004062604

Two sticks, two sticks,
Maybelle played with two sticks,
Two bounce-like-a-kangaroo sticks,
Two drum-dee-dum-dee-doo sticks!

Two two-times-two-is-four sticks,
Two on-a-wooden-floor sticks,

Two beat-them-on-a-door sticks,

Two make-your-parents-sore sticks!

They said, "Girl, stop that fake drum,
That shaking-us-awake drum,
That giving-us-an-ache drum,
That this-we-cannot-take drum!"

But Maybelle wanted SOME drum,
A kettle, snare, not humdrum,
A drum-dee-dum-dee-dum drum,
Oh, any funky fun drum!

She ran off to a new beat,
A hip-hopping, shoe-by-shoe beat,
A Maybelle-through-and-through beat,
A wake-up-the-bayou beat!

Her sticks picked out a neat beat,
A rake-the-fence-repeat beat,
A drumming-on-the-street beat
Faster than her feet beat!

She played upon a bare log,
A cross-me-if-you-dare log,
A rotten I-don't-care log,
A Maybelle-doesn't-scare log!

Her sticks were making potholes,
Swiss-cheesy scattershot holes,

Big would-she-fall-or-not holes,

Till there was nothing BUT holes!

She fell into a vile swamp,
A slimy, crocodile swamp,
A reptiles-by-the-mile swamp,
A do-your-best-to-smile swamp!

And she had only two sticks,
Her tried and trusty true sticks,

Two beat-them-where-they-chew sticks,
Two bee-bop-a-doo-dang-doo sticks!

Each tooth rang with a round sound,
Each cavity, profound sound,
A deep-down-underground sound
In crocodile-surround sound!

She played a toothy dance tune,
A crocodile-romance tune,
A keep-them-in-a-trance tune,
A please-give-me-a-chance tune!

Eleven scaly tails swung.
Ten thousand shiny scales swung.
The females and the males swung.
Their clicking, clacking nails swung!

She played that grinning pack home.
With pride she brought them back home,
All dancing on the track home
To every click and clack home!

Her folks and neighbors woke up.
They jumped with every stroke up.
When Maybelle's music broke up,
She clicked her sticks and spoke up:

"I finally found the right drum,
A ringing, singing, bright drum,
A crocodile-won't-bite drum,
A bing-bang-dynamite drum!"

Her parents had to cheer now.
They wouldn't interfere now.
"Choose any drum, my dear, now.
Just get them out of here NOW!"

So Maybelle got a real drum,
A big calypso steel drum,
A musical, ideal drum,
A pinging, swinging-feel drum!

She played it with her two sticks,
Two lollipop-like new sticks,
Two bounce-like-a-kangaroo sticks,
Two drum-dee-dum-dee-doo sticks!

Now she could ping and pong sticks,
Ding as well as dong sticks,
Bim-bam all day long sticks
And never lose her song . . .

Bing banga doobie dabba . . . so long!